PUMPKIN MAGIC

written by
Ed Masessa

illustrated by
Nate Wragg

Cartwheel Books
Scholastic • New York

ISBN 978-1-338-56332-0
10 9 8 7 6 5 4 3 2 1   20 21 22 23 24

Printed in the U.S.A.   40
First printing 2020
Book design by Steve Ponzo

Lonely pumpkin on a stair, glowing in the chilly air.
Moonbeam magic lights a spark. Pumpkin rises in the dark!

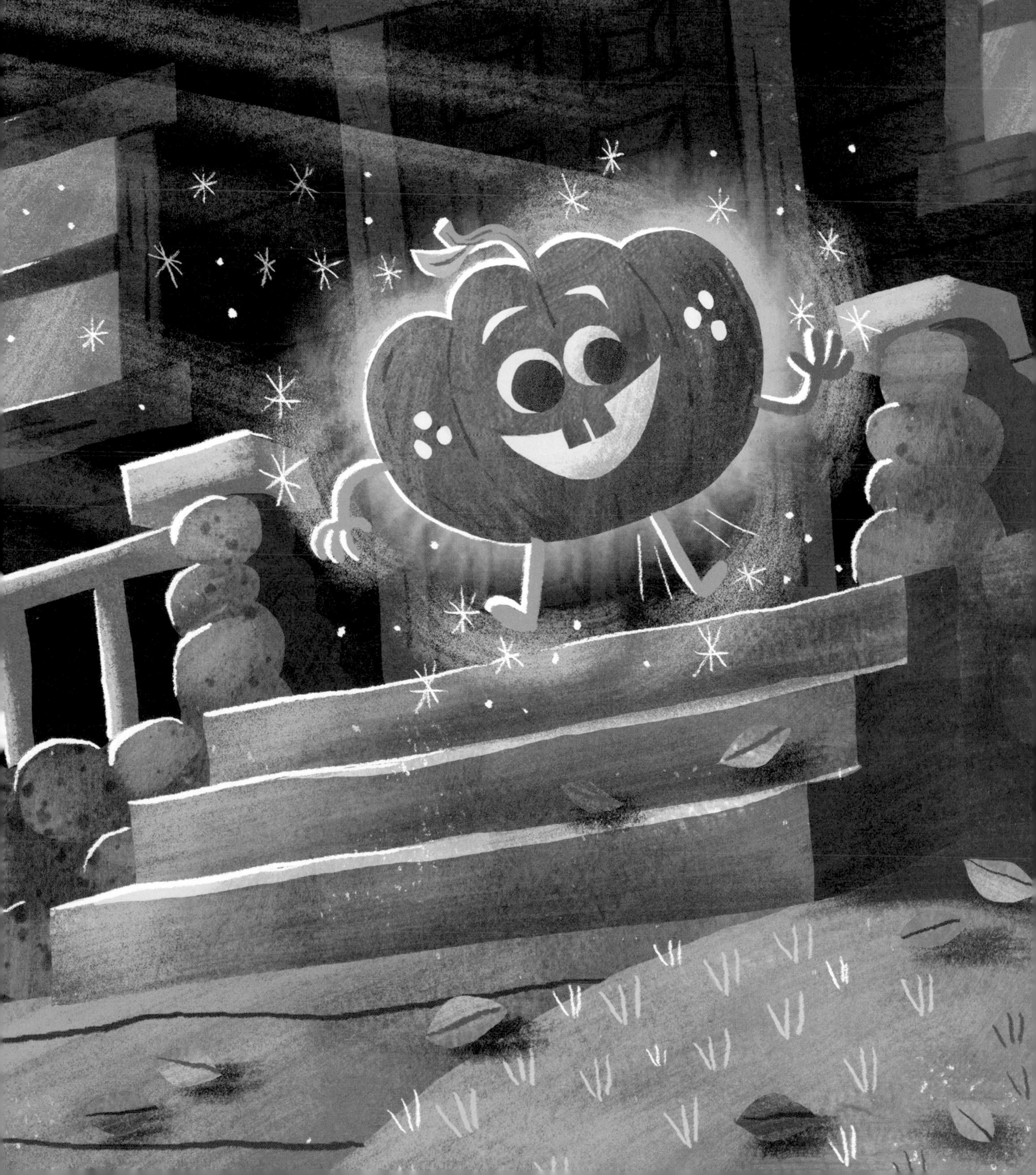

Pumpkin bouncing down the street,
looking for a friend to greet.

Pumpkin's heart begins to soar!
Pumpkin patch with friends galore!

Pumpkin magic in the air.
Moonbeams touching everywhere!

Pumpkins with your eyes so bright,
won't you light the field tonight?

Happy pumpkin grinning wide.
Friends are playing side by side.

Stacking pumpkins one by one.
Falling pumpkins having fun!

Pumpkins round, pumpkins square.
Pumpkins in their underwear.

Knobby pumpkins white and green,
bouncing on a trampoline!

Pumpkins at a fairy ball.

Who's the fairest of them all?

Pumpkins marching six by six.
Drumming pumpkins banging sticks.

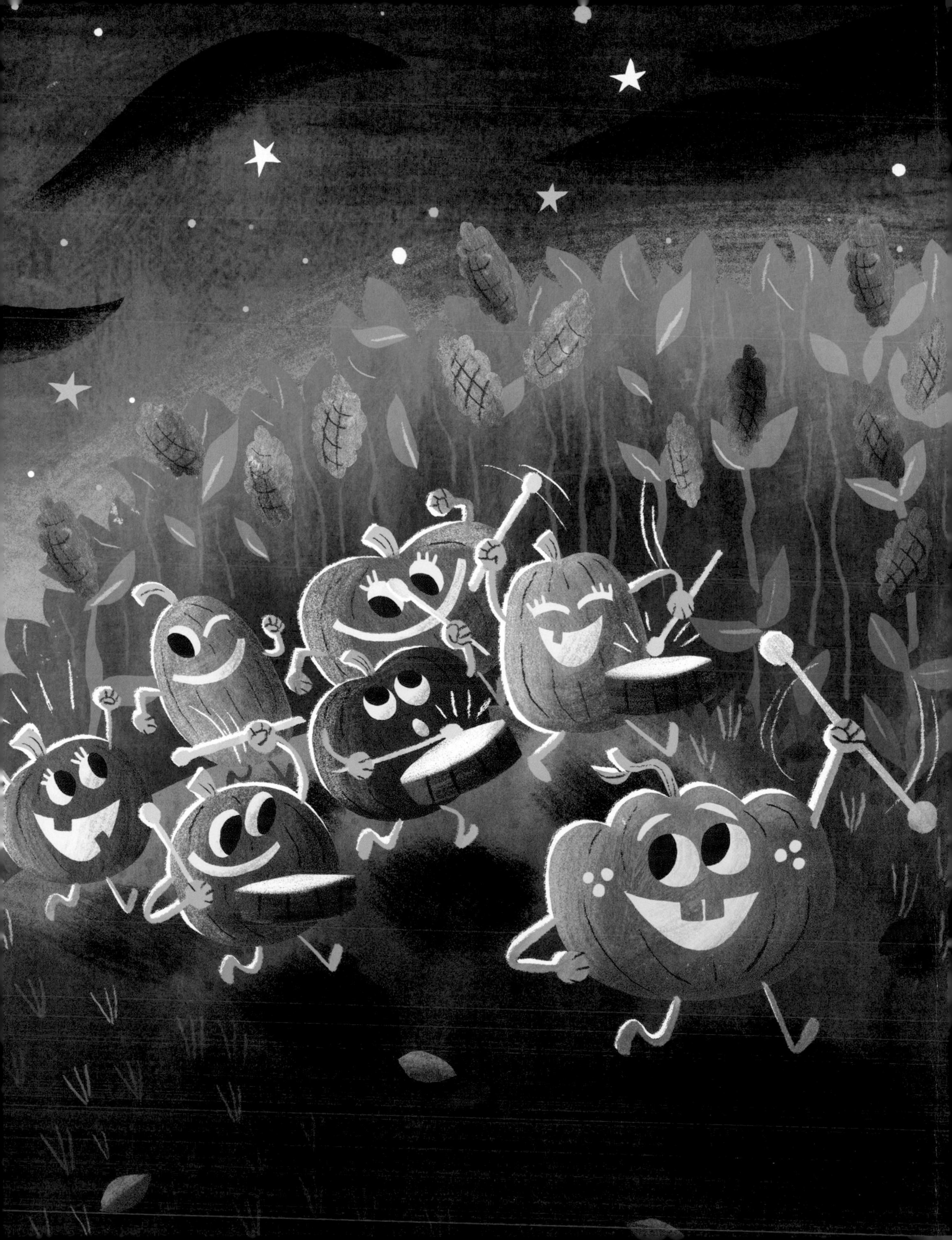

Vines for hats and corn for feet.

Costumed pumpkins — trick or treat!

Seeds are flying, targets hit.
How far can a pumpkin spit?

Goopy mud pies taking flight.
Naughty pumpkins shout "Food fight!"

Pumpkin faces downright scary.
All but one — he's just hairy.

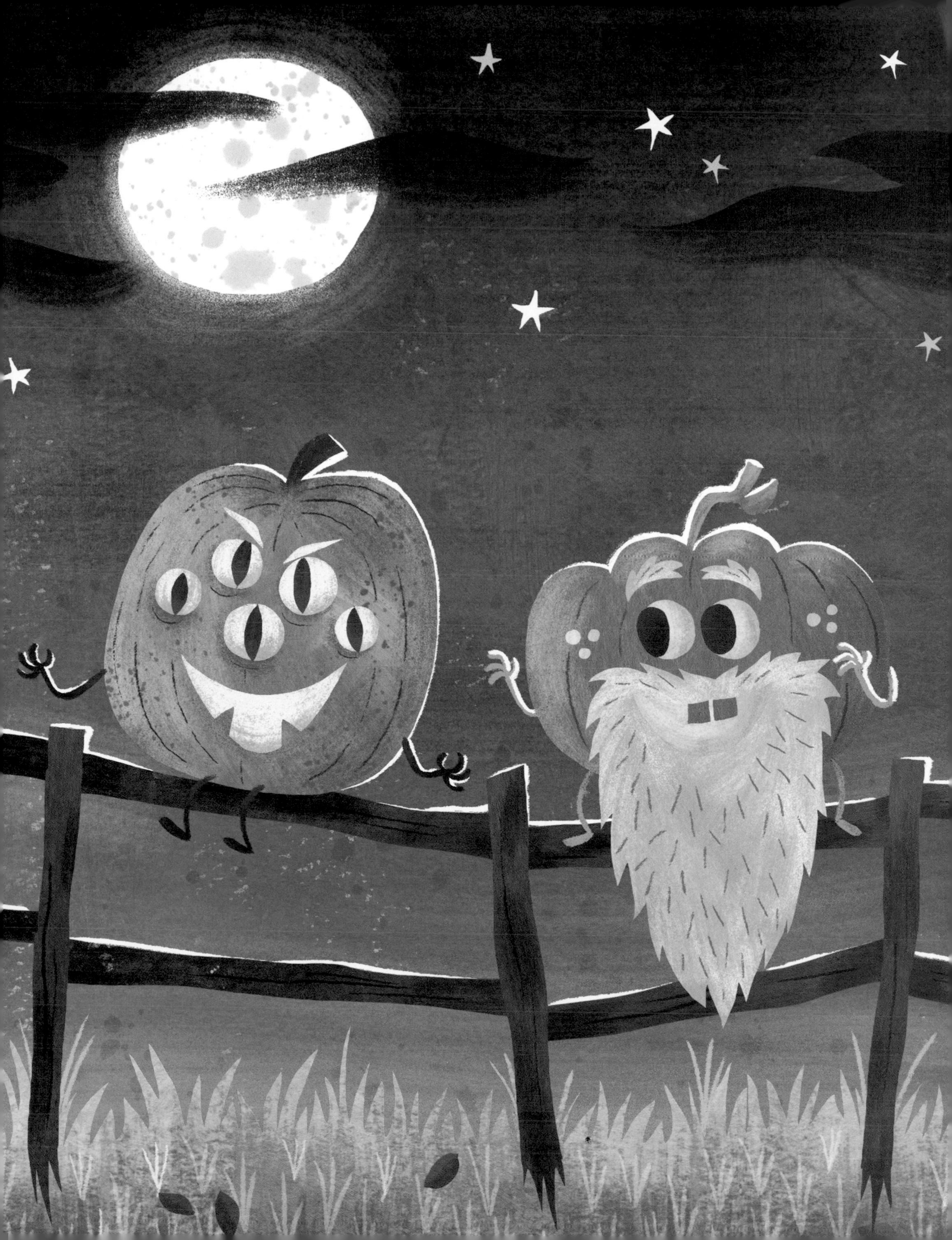

Clowny pumpkins quite bizarre.
Ten squeeze in a pumpkin car!

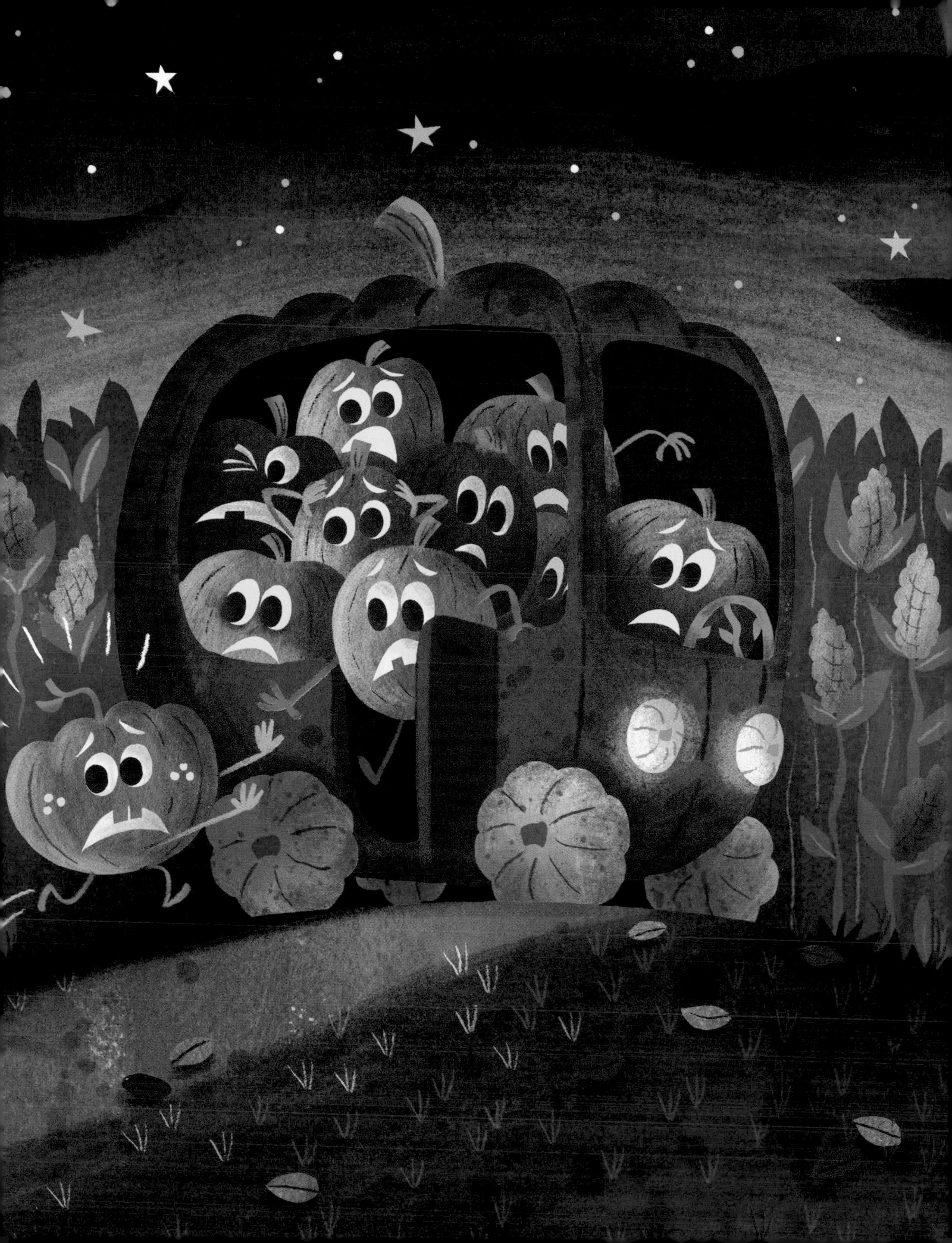

Witchy pumpkin, warty nose.
Flies on broomstick with the crows.

Wizard pumpkin waves a wand . . .
Oops! She landed in a pond.

Morning's near; they see the sun.
Time for play is almost done.

Just one thing is left to do.
Pumpkin leads them two by two.

Pumpkins rolling down the street.
Climbing stairs to take a seat.

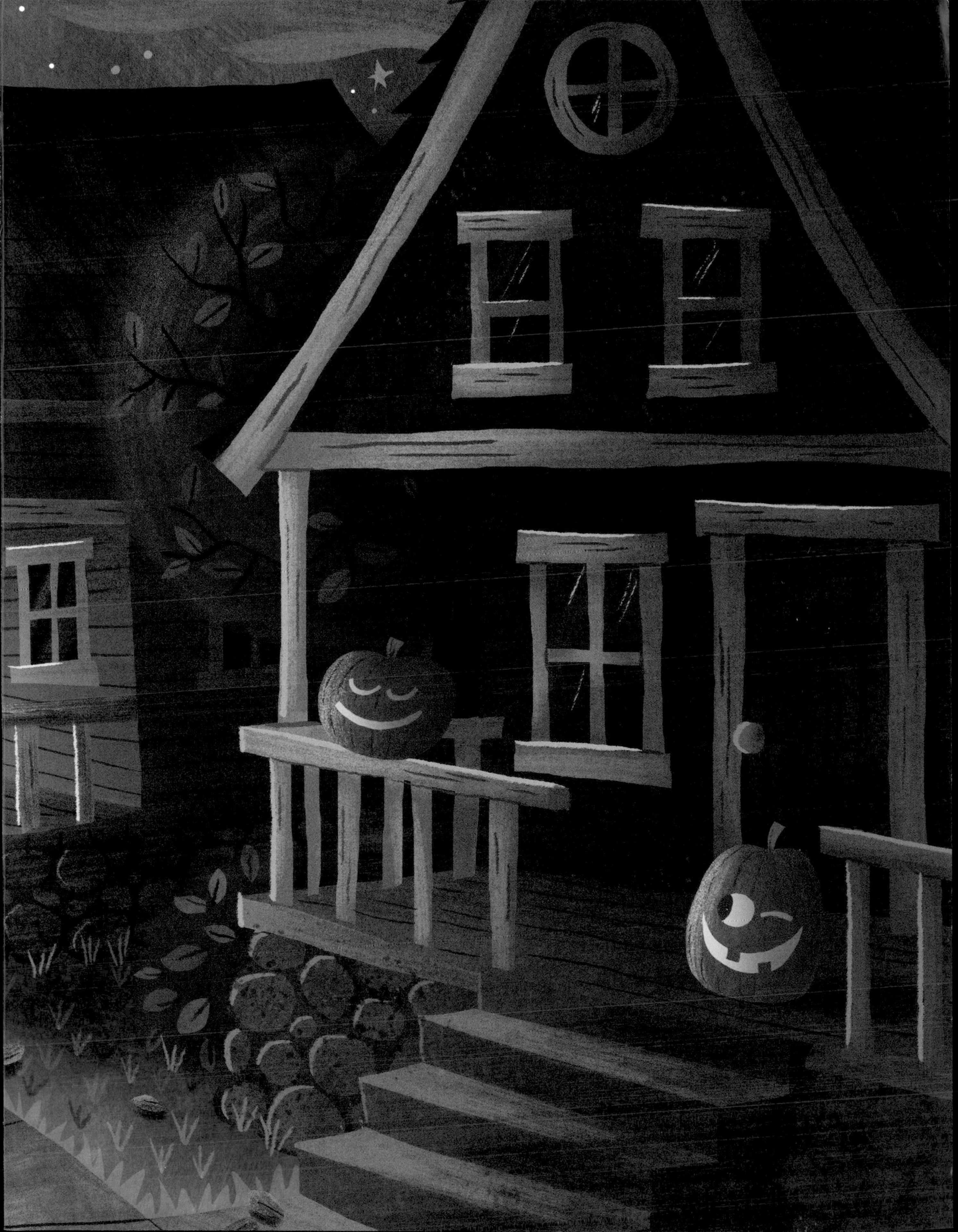

Candles out, it's getting late.
Patient pumpkins lie and wait . . .

Until the moonbeams shine just right . . .

And pumpkins romp
all through the night.